QUEEN OF THE MAY

For Abigail, always Queen of the May

S.K.

For Mickey,
for lifting the snared and the sorrowful
with your wings and your singing

Thank you Ed Young,
for your generous inspiration and
contagious aura of well-being

P.B.

Library of Congress Cataloging-in-Publication Data
Kroll, Steven.
Queen of the May / Steven Kroll ; illustrated by Patience
Brewster.—1st ed.
p. cm.
Summary: Because of Sylvie's goodness, her wicked stepmother and
stepsister are vanquished and she becomes Queen of the May.
ISBN 0-8234-1004-8
[1. May Day—Fiction. 2. Fairy tales.] I. Brewster, Patience,
ill. II. Title.
mi8.K912Qu   1993   92-16393   CIP   AC
[E]—dc20

QUEEN OF THE MAY

by STEVEN KROLL

ILLUSTRATED by PATIENCE BREWSTER

HOLIDAY HOUSE / NEW YORK

Sylvie lived in a village with her stepmother and her stepsister, Gudrun. While they lay around and slept, Sylvie did all the chores on the farm.

Even on holidays, Sylvie had to work. But this year, when May Day came, she wanted to finish early. The girl who brought the most beautiful flowers to the village green would be chosen Queen of the May. Sylvie yearned to pick a bouquet and join the celebration.

While Gudrun and her stepmother snored, Sylvie got up at first light, milked the cow, gathered the eggs, and swept the house. Then she put away her broom and got out her cape.

Her stepmother yawned and stretched. "Where are you going?"

"To pick flowers for May Day," said Sylvie.

"You can't!" said Gudrun. "We have more chores for you to do today."

Sylvie was so sad, she couldn't eat. She watched Gudrun and her stepmother wolf down their porridge. When they were satisfied, her stepmother slammed down her spoon and said, "Now go out to the barn. Wrap twigs of mountain ash around the milk pail and the butter churn. Cut a hawthorn bough, hang it from the front door, and scatter primroses across our front steps. We must protect the farm from the evil spirits who come out on May Day."

As Sylvie reached the barn, she looked over her shoulder. Gudrun was plodding down the path to the fields.

The fields were bursting with flowers nodding their heads, waiting to be picked. But Gudrun chose only this one and that one and never the prettiest. Perhaps, she thought, she would do better in the field on the other side of the woods.

Gudrun hurried toward the woods. As she reached the edge, she heard a pitiful squeaking sound.

Near a wild blackberry bush, a chipmunk was caught in a snare.

"Please," said the chipmunk, "would you help me?"

"No!" said Gudrun. "I'm in too much of a hurry!"

She went on into the woods and came to a stream. A beaver dam had broken, and water was rushing through, carrying sticks and mud along with it.

"Please help me," cried the beaver. "The water is washing away my house."

Gudrun turned up her nose. "I can't help you. I have more important things to do!"

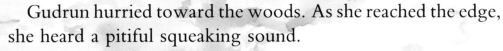

She kept walking until she came to a very tall tree. She could hear the weak fluttering of wings. Looking up, she saw a large crow trapped among the branches.

"Please help me," said the crow. "I'm stuck."

"You clumsy creature," said Gudrun. "I have no time for you!"

She hurried away from the woods into the field beyond.

By the time Sylvie had hung the hawthorn bough over the front door and scattered the primroses across the steps, the morning was almost over. Still, she hoped there would be time to gather a small bouquet before the Queen of the May was chosen.

"I'd like to take a walk in the fields," Sylvie told her stepmother.

"You must weed the garden and prepare the soup for dinner first," came the reply.

There's so much to do, I'll never have time to gather flowers, Sylvie thought. But she hurried through her last two chores, and as her stepmother dozed before the fire, she ran into the fields.

Sylvie saw the special beauty of the flowers in a way that Gudrun had not. Very soon she had gathered a gorgeous bouquet.

As she was finishing, she heard a squeal from the edge of the woods. She rushed over, and there was the chipmunk, still caught in the snare.

"You poor thing," Sylvie said, and freed him.

The chipmunk sat up on his hind feet.

"Thank you," he said. "If you're ever in trouble, look right beneath your nose."

Then he dashed into the woods.

Sylvie followed, thinking she would go only a little way.

But almost at once she heard the beaver's cries, and saw before her the stream and the broken dam.

Sylvie waded into the rushing water. She began replacing the missing branches and logs until the dam was as good as new.

"You have been so kind," said the beaver. "If you're ever in trouble, look right beneath your nose."

Sylvie smiled. Then, from deep in the woods, she heard the shrieks of the crow.

She ran until she came to the very tall tree. She saw the crow still struggling and climbed to the branch just below him. Then she shook the branches that were pinning his wings, and the crow soared free.

"If you're ever in trouble," he said as he flew away, "look right beneath your nose."

By this time Sylvie could see the field on the other side of the woods. She hurried there to pick her last few flowers.

As soon as she came out of the woods, a rope cage fell on top of her.

She struggled to get free, but the ropes held her fast. She was still struggling when a hag appeared. "Be still," said the hag. "You won't be going anywhere now."

Sylvie fought and kicked, but the hag carried her off to her hut. There was a girl sitting by the hearth.

"Gudrun!" said Sylvie. "Why are *you* here?"

Gudrun smirked and turned away.

"I have been watching both of you secretly," said the hag. "You are an ungrateful girl, Sylvie. You don't deserve to be Queen of the May. *Gudrun* will be the queen!"

She took Gudrun's hand, and the two of them left for the village. Sylvie began to cry.

Then she remembered what the animals
had told her—and looked right beneath
her nose. The beaver was wriggling through
the ropes, gnawing them apart.
The chipmunk was licking away her tears.

She raced outside.
The crow was perched
on a fencepost,
an elegant white dress
billowing below him.

"Put this on," he said,
"and I'll fly you to the village.
There's still time."

He spread his wings and stretched.
Sylvie climbed onto his back.
They flew over hills and
valleys and fields and houses.

The crow landed on the village green. Gudrun was standing by the Maypole, about to be crowned Queen of the May. Her mother—Sylvie's wicked stepmother— stood beside her. A small boy noticed Sylvie and her flowers. "Look!" he shouted, "look!"

Sylvie quietly held her bouquet as the crowd surrounded her. Two children placed the crown on Sylvie's head and bowed before her. Then they took her by the hand and led her to the Maypole. Everyone danced around it, celebrating the return of spring.

At the same time, the crow swooped down on Gudrun and her mother. Flapping and pecking, he chased them for miles, and as far as anyone knows, they're running still.

As for the hag, she disappeared into the mountains forever, and Sylvie had all the happiness she wanted for the rest of her life.